Where Innocence
—— Ends ——

Shinetaha Saincila

authorHOUSE®

AuthorHouse™
1663 Liberty Drive
Bloomington, IN 47403
www.authorhouse.com
Phone: 1 (800) 839-8640

Published by AuthorHouse 06/14/2016

ISBN: 978-1-5246-1416-4 (sc)
ISBN: 978-1-5246-1415-7 (e)

Library of Congress Control Number: 2016909731

Print information available on the last page.

To my father Jeanpaul,
To my adoptive mother Guerda, and my godmother
Mary-france,
Along with my two cousins who has always believed in
me, Othon and Yvener.
And to my best friend from High School, Tahira.
Miss you kid.

PROLOGUE

Marcus the political drug lord stands still watching us run. It was an exercise that we have to do every day, every morning when we wake up at 4 AM before sunrise. We suppose to run in circle 30 times, non-stop. If one of us stops running, one of the rebel guards will pull his revolver out and shoot us in the head. We have no choice but to keep strong to survive.

"Hurry up!" He shouts. "Faster. Faster." He looks in his gold watch for the clock. "It's almost time boys."

We run and run, and run. Till we'd it made to 30. We all collapse on the ground when we reach 30. Most of us were exhausted and some of us try to breath.

"What's the plan for the day?" I ask Mathieu.

Mathieu is a senior here. He wasn't new here like most us. Beside he was one of the first kidnapped and chosen children there in the group.

"Valcoub" He answers with his olive green eyes, while he bites his lower lip.

Valcoub is one of the mountainous villages in Valmont. Valmont is a country located in the Central

America, neighboring the Caribbean Sea, where lays the countries Cuba, Jamaica, Haiti, and the Dominican Republic. But however though, Valmont is surrounded by the border of Costa Rica and Panama.

Valmont is a small island too. It was also abandoned during the late 1700s, based on supernatural phenomena that had occurred here. People find it to be a land of evil, because it has mysterious ghosts hunting and unexplained stories. The villagers left the place and moved either north outside the island or south. No one ever came back here again, until in the 1970s a group of religious Christian missionaries settle here in the supernatural island forest paradise. They worked here on plantation, steels, production, minerals, creates a government and industries.

At first, Valmont was an independent country. It worked hard to get itself there. Within just 28 years we have skylines and great city passage lanes. It was such a Christian country, but then greed took over the people of the government. They seek to advance the country into a political chaotic country.

The people were overreacted to this new nature that was taking over the Christian island. But the government would shut them off act against, making most of the majority population to live in poverty or do efforts to expand the country's wealth. Then autocracy grew and illegal drugs took over and became a big trade. Drug lords rule among us, and the government express lies to us bluffing about how they stand in our side. But it seems like they're just fighting for themselves, while they battle against the drug lords. And that's how drug lords rule the people of the country; well I could say the economy within the black market.

Drug lords shoots and kills people in the streets. Even innocents became their preys and their victims, mostly their slave boys like I am. Day and night it is a war; everybody lives at risks. And government military take no pity from anyone, but engage themselves in the middle of the war.

Anyway, since I introduced the story of Valmont, now let me introduce myself. My name is Kasich Blond, an English descent born in Valmont. I'm actually 12 and I was once kidnapped by an illegal drug gang called, the *Sanarina*. They took me away one day when they invaded the school that I used to attend, *The Young Apostles Elementary School*. I was about the age of 9 that time, I was in 5 Grade, and I was actually called the class clown throughout the school. Teachers used to yelled at me, and get irritated all the time, especially when I interrupted the class with a joke.

As for my family, I wasn't much loved by them. But I'm pretty sure they have a soft spot for me. They get so possessive by the way life work now in Valmont, their only desires for their children is for us to fulfill their dreams not ours, especially for us to become Doctors or Politicians to fit the society of rich people. Every time they asked me what profession that I wanted to do with my life. I would answer them that I just wanted to be me, do me, and myself only. Then that's when they started reject me, except for my two older brothers who is their puppet and my baby sister, Lela who just know nothing at all.

In all my family, the only person I ever loved is my grandmother Nola and my baby sister Lela. They never really think of me as a bad child, and my baby sister always treats me equal like everybody else. She is a good soul.

When my parents spoke in front of me, they would either swear and make disrespectful gestured in front of me. While it comes to my siblings they would treated them with respect, and for them I was completely invisible in the house. I was nothing. Now that I am kidnapped and force to be a slave fighter for certain drug lords, they'll probably miss me. But as long as I am alive I will fight to survive, and try to my way to freedom.

****

Marcus the drug lord told us to get back to our tents and grab our equipment, because this morning is going to be another busy morning. Let me guess. Robbing people and killing them. I roll my eyes as I walk inside my tent. I grab my 33 military SWAT gun. It was very heavy for me to hold before, but now I got used to it. I also grab a small photo of me and my sister Lela, when she was three when I was kidnapped. Now she's probably 6 and I guess she won't remember me, because she was a toddler when I was around. I place the photo on my jeans pocket. I took my knives with me, since I do not know if I would survive another day or not, and even though I do I would have to take what's necessary most to me, because we might never come back to the same location again.

CHAPTER 1

Valcoub, we finally made it there. When we arrived, a little girl in a blue uniform school skirt, a back pack on her back, and some fancy Adidas sneaker. Stands on the small side walk of the narrow lanes of the street. Her hazel brown eyes stare straight into my own innocent blue eyes. I felt splendid and astonish of her sneakers, I haven't had a good pair of sneaker in years, and I want hers. But by the moment we get off the pickup truck, the girl sight already disappears. Oh how great! Now I lost her.

Marcus gets out of his truck, he looks at each one of us and then smiles to the ones that look funny to him on his regards. He looks at those who are anxious and nervous, while he curses them badly, telling them that they are weak kids from weak women wombs.

I try to ignore him swear, but I can't just cover my ears with fingers or look away, if do he would either kill me or injure me. So, I have no choice.

Finally, he comes close to me, right in front of me facing me man versus man. I stood there frozen and numb. He looks straight at me with his murderous gray eyes. He bent down and spit to the ground near my feet. He did not laugh nor smile, but curiosity mark his face, while he passes his dirty finger through his short blonde and gray hair.

"What's your name again, boy?" He asks.

"Kasich" I said deeply. "Kasich Blond, master."

"Mr. Blond." He slightly smirks. "I barely heard your voice. How come you never speak?"

"I do, sir."

"Then, why are you so mute?" He shouts. "Did the Sanarina cut your tongue out of your mouth?"

All the kids laugh and giggle with their crooked teeth, based on Marcus remarks toward me. I felt embarrassed and upset, I wanted to shoot them all and leave.

"No, sir" I stammer, as my body tremble and my breathing becomes heavy.

"Do you want me to cut your tongue out of your mouth?" He laughs.

"No, sir" I praise him. "Please don..." Then a gunshot from the air interrupts us.

Marcus quickly draws his gun to the direction of the gunshot. But it got quiet.

Marcus gave us all a signal. He points out to one of his slave or rebel boy name Flinch, 21 years-old with tattoos cover his back and arms, and full of piercing in his face. Two piercing place on each of his eyebrows, one in the bottom of his lip, two on his cheekbones.

To be honest I found his appearance to be hideous and scary.

Marcus told Flinch and his teammates to go west. Which Flinch did follow along with his mates that has five men who is around the age of 20s and early 30s, and three children who was around my age.

Then Marcus order Mathieu his most trusted slave boy and closes friend. He told Mathieu to go east along with his teammates, which is the team that I'm in. It was only five of us in Mathieu team; three of us are children and two teens among us, plus Mathieu who is a pre-teen, which makes up six of us together. Mathieu nods at us as we follow Marcus, and Marcus went along with some rebels in the north side where the gunshot has been heard.

I went with Mathieu and the others to the east. Which was a big area, and I feel scare as hell going there. I mean what if I get shot? I will never see another day again, another sunset in my life, and neither see my goals process.

"Draw your pistols boys." Mathieu order us in action. We all did what he told us. I in the other hand, full up my gun with those hard bullets, and whisper to myself. "Mother of Christ keeps me safe." Then the sounds of gunshots start to erupt.

I quickly split up with Mathieu and the other boys as they start shooting while they run from the streets to corridors. I hop up behind a house wall, breathing heavily. I sneak my head quick looking around to see if there is anyone shooting at my direction, but didn't see anyone. But one sniper stands on a blue cripple house roof top, hiding himself-there while a tip of his gun shows. But he doesn't take any notice of it.

I know I have to kill the other guy in order to survive, so I pull up my revolver in his direction and pull the trigger. The sound of the bullet boom in my ears, almost cause me to become deaf, and it trembles my veins as it pulled off.

The bullet hit him in the head causing a small hole on his forehead pouring out blood, as he collapses on the ground in seconds. Then he falls out of the roof lifeless.

Brandon, who saw this with his big dark brown eyes, gave me a thumbs up and run to my side to join.

"Screw this place, I don't like it." He murmurs under his breath, while he stands next to me behind the house wall where I hide. "I don't want to die."

"Unh" I sight. "That's what all newbie says."

"Shut up!" He rolls his eyes. "You'll be the last person to say this."

"Well, then how come you haven't pulled a trigger?" I raise an eyebrow.

He shook his head and smiles. Brandon is a boy that is half born Syrian and Nigerian descent. He is new to this war, well I could say new to this fighter life. I also found him to be a scary cater, I don't know how he survive and how the Conovhi buy him.

The Conovhi is Marcus gang, well when the Sanarina kidnapped me. I was trained as a child warrior and I was one of the top rank fighters among the children there. Well to be a slaves to those drug lords, and make them sales us for good money, you have to be good. And the person who buy us will become our owner or master should I say.

That is how life is here in Valmont. And no one can do anything about that, except the government who are fighting against them can. But they haven't made any liberation to any of us, and when they get into a fight with us. We are either killed or survive, they don't care about who is a slave and who isn't. For them once a man creates an army, the army became just like their master's.

"Let's go." I told Brandon.

"Go where?" He curiously asks.

"In the blue house where the guy I shot was in."

He laughs and shake his head in denials. "Are you crazy?" He says backing up. "I don't know about you, but I am not going. What makes you think there might be another sniper inside?"

"Shit!" I swear under breath.

I draw my rifle and get ready to move, Brandon then goes behind me following my lead, because he knew for sure that I am about to leave him here by himself. And his scary self would not move anywhere till somebody come and shoots him.

I look at the house while I walk in front it, Brandon walks behind me guarding for any suspicious enemies that might come to attack us.

I ran to the front door banging the door with my feet, till it breaks open. Before I got inside the house,

Brandon the scary cat already flew himself there before I got the chance to. I shook my head smiling how his scary self is such an hilarious rat; I held my guns looking around for any target. Till I heard Brandon screams. I look around to see to whom he was screaming at. Then I saw this man who probably on his mid-40, he was hiding behind the door filling out bullets in his gun.

"Shoot him!" I shout to Brandon. He did try to shoot the guy, but he misses. So, I quickly point my gun at the guy and pull the trigger. Then, the guy grunts in pain as the bullet hit him in his stomach, and I pull out a trigger again this time hit him straight in the brain.

The guy collapses on the floor. Then, when I turn around to Brandon, he stood there beside me with his gun held in his hand, while he tremble in fright. I look him up from head to toe and smirks, because he looks funny being scare.

CHAPTER 2

In the blue house me and Brandon gather some golds and jewels and hide it inside our pocket and boots, anywhere that is possible for it to fit. I think stealing them is a good idea because it might cost us a fortune one day, if only we made it out of this slavery life.

"Promise me you won't tell Marcus and the others." Brandon said to me.

"This is between us not them." I gave the pinky finger.

Why would he expect me to tell Marcus and the others about the golds and the jewels? I'm trying to make it out of here just like he is. But how will I? Maybe the sunset will teach me how to, but I need direction first. I wish the moon could at night gives me a map when I am sleeping.

"We have to go quick!" Brandon cries anxiously, interrupting my thought.

"Go where?" I ask.

"Back to Mathieu," He answers while putting the jewels inside his underwear. "They're getting into this area in a minute."

I shook my head unbelief seeing how Brandon such a damn child, these jewels could injure his manhood. What is he thinking?

"How do you know that they're coming?" I curiously ask, while raising an eyebrow at him. Because this boy probably seeing things, that he's probably imagined.

Since the front door is still open, I peak my head out to see while holding my gun. But see none.

"No one is coming."

"Go look in the bathroom window in the back of house." He says.

I did what he said, and then my heart started to race when I saw Mathieu and two other boys from the team heading near the place, but one was missing. Maybe he dies or finds a hideout somewhere.

I burst into the kitchen and open the stove gas letting the helium air invade the house. I ran outside of the house with my gun held in my hand, Brandon did the same. But we were surprise to see the same girl with the Adidas sneakers run behind us. Brandon point his revolver at her as she runs for her life, but I lower his gun letting the girl go.

"Why did you do that for?" Brandon sighs.

"She is not an enemy," I yell at him, trying to make him understand. "She's just a frightening."

He sucks his teeth turning his back around indignantly, then he hands me a lighter from his jeans pocket. I light it up and throw it inside the house, then the house explodes with a violent and scary boom of sound while it trembles inside my stomach.

The force of the explosion is so strong that it velocity shakes the ground causing me and Brandon to collapse on the ground.

"What was that?" A familiar voice asks behind me.

I turn around seeing Mathieu and the two boys' stand behind us drawing their rifles in panic.

"It was some men inside." Brandon told him. "I guess they were enemies."

Mathieu nods his head then he looks at me lying on the ground, he gave me a disguise look and told me to get up. I did what he ordered. I and Brandon follow him as he walks in front us leading us along with his boys.

Brandon look at me in scares, I put my index finger toward my lip telling him to hush him up. Then I look up seeing a bunch of military snipers coming toward us with their gun in their hands. Mathieu and his boys quickly grab their rifles and started shooting at them.

I instantly run and look around searching for safety to save myself. There was a broken car abandon near the sidewalk. I hop on top of the car, and slip to its side where it blocks me away from the battle. Brandon did the same.

Mathieu stood there behind a wall of a corridor, shooting at the military snipers as they hit back at him and his boys. Mathieu shouts out to me and Brandon to come out from our hide out and help them. I ignore him, while the bullets sounds are booming.

"Shoot him." I said to Brandon.

"Shoot who?" He curiously asks. I press Brandon's rifle on his chest as try to let my eyes tell him.

Brandon gives me a baffle look; I pound him in the arm. "Come on do it!"

"I can't!" He replies in a loud tone so that I could hear him behind those noisy gunshots. "Marcus will kill us."

I roll my eyes at him. "Screw you, stupid." I said. Then I peak my head out a little bit, and fix my gun at Mathieu direction while he gives me a sign of to shoot at those military snipers. I ignore his sign and pull the trigger on him, but it hit him in his right knee. He grunts in pain holding his knee to cover the blood.

Brandon curses me out toward my action. "You a wick punk, you know that?"

"Oh says the scary cat." I laugh.

One of the boys that stood by Mathieu side shoots at me, but I quickly move away before the bullet got the chance. Then I point my gun at him and shoot him in the chest as he hit the ground lifeless.

The other boy that stood by Mathieu started shooting at us non-stops, but the car kept us safe. I grab Brandon and lower our head as the mad boy keep on shooting. He then stops shooting, I peak my head out slowly expect to see him loading his gun, but he wasn't there except for Mathieu's laying on the ground shooting at the snipers.

I look at Mathieu pointing my gun once more. I meditate my mind on him and then shoot him in the ear as the bullet passes through his brain and kills him.

I grab Brandon in the arm and run with him as the snipers are pointing their guns toward us. We run as quickly as possible so that no bullet can't hit us.

The little girl with the Adidas sneaker stands near a narrow corridor, where the walls seems a little distant from each other.

"Follow me." She says as she run in the middle of the corridor.

I did the same with Brandon as we follow her. She leads us to in the middle of a wood near a river. She hands me and Brandon some food which is supposed to be her school lunch from her backpack.

The wind blows her blonde hair while it covers her brown eyes. For instance, she looks like an angel straight out of heaven. I ignore my food while Brandon seats there eating like a pig. My eyes stay in hers through every move she does, fixing the books in her backpack.

"Where are you from?" She asks me.

"Morentzo" I answer.

Yeah I'm from Morentzo that is my city, the city where I used to live with my family. But now I have no place except for life itself.

"What about your friend?" She asks.

"I don't know about him." I reply to her. "But right now he is hungry I guess." I smile to her; she did the same and all the sudden I felt a butterfly laid inside my stomach. Therefore, her smile was illumining.

"Thank you for your hospitality." Brandon thanks her.

"Maria!" A woman voice shrieks through the wood. The girl turns around in panic zipping her backpack.

I was confused, why she is so in panic? But she put her backpack on her back and said. "I have to go."

"Where are you going?" I ask her while I hold her arm. But she pushes my hand away, I felt remorseful as she did.

"My mother is worry about me." She said and then run out of the woods.

"But you didn't even catch my name?" I yell.

"I will one day." She said back.

I stood there all sad; I couldn't believe this girl left me and Brandon here without her asking for our names. I mean she just save my life; she could have stay for a couple of minutes.

"I guess someone have a crush." Brandon smirks.

"Shut up!" I slap in the back of the head.

"Ouch!" He screams. "That hurt you know."

"Yep I know." I laugh.

CHAPTER 3

As I was seating there in the wood with Brandon by my side eating the food that Maria had gave us, someone caught me and Brandon in the back of the neck hard. The hand seems like a man hand, it feels old and sturdy.

"Caught you now you little punks." The voice says.

"Let go of me!" Brandon yells. "Let go."

I turn my head around without even looking at the guy in the face, and punch him in the stomach. He gasps in pain and let go of me and Brandon, while he holds his stomach for support. I try to grab my rifle, but I heard the voice said. "You punch like a little bitch."

I turn my head to look at the face while I my fingers touch the rifle on the floor, it was Flinch. Of course he would've told me that I punch like a little bitch, because he thinks I'm just an innocent kid. But while I was about to pull the trigger, he punches me in the face with his hard knuckles hand and everything faded black.

In a moment, I feel something seems soft; I open my eyes to see where I am. Then I panic in fright seeing myself looking at the ground. I was far, far away from the earth itself where the clouds fade the view of Valmont and it rivers. Oh my god I am high in the air I said to myself, nothing holds me back. I start to tremble but at the same time happy. Then I feel a cold hand passes its fingers my face. I close my eyes letting the fingers twirl in my face. It was comfortable and softs, I wanted this forever. I open my eyes to see who it was and all suddenly I felt happy. Happy like a child again, not as those slave soldiers' children that has lost their innocents, but like a normal child. It was Maria's. Her hands were twirling at my face. But a voice in the sound of thunder interrupts us. "Get up you punk!" The voice said.

Then Maria's hand let go of my face. Her face expression changes, she was frightening. I held my hand to grab her's but she ran. And the voice keeps on repeating itself again, and again. Suddenly I felt like someone was kicking me in my legs. I try to look for the person who was kicking me when everything around me starts to fade black, but I couldn't see anyone. Then all the sudden my heart beat fast and kept on beating, then I open my eyes the first person I see is Flinch with those piercing in his lips shouting at me. He was saying something, but I could not hear him. Therefore, his voice seems to be far away, then I realize that I was dreaming about Maria touching my face with her fingers, and in reality I was on the ground and while Flinch is kicking me hard in my legs and in my stomach.

"Get up you punk." Flinch said sharply by grabbing me on my collar shirt. As he holds my color shirt, my eyes and his eyes met, we both breathe heavily in anger.

"Leave me alone!" I said spitting on his face.

He throws me off the ground and wept those spits that I left in his face with his hands in disgust. He was about to punch me, but Marcus pull him out of my sight.

"Where's Mathieu?" Marcus asks, while he puts his dirty hand in my throat.

"I don't know." I cry feeling the pressure of his fingertips trying to choke me.

"What'd you mean, you don't know?" He says in a shallow voice.

"I don't know, sir" I hold his dirty fighting to find air.

"We found him dead in Valcoub." Brandon interrupts by bringing himself into the quarrel. "He was shot in the head, he even had a wounded gunshot in the knee too."

"Really?" Marcus curiously asks Brandon while he let go of my neck. But Brandon took a step back, however though I could smell him, he smells like fear. Like the devil is coming to get him.

"How come you guys didn't take the body?"

"It was too late, sir." I said to him. Making him pay his full attentions to me, instead of Brandon. "The soldiers were shooting at us like crazy. We couldn't have the chance to take the body."

"Hmm...," Marcus hummed under his breath. "Something doesn't seem right."

"What is it, master?" A boy asks. While everybody starts to bring questions out of nowhere.

I look at Brandon's eyes who looks back at me. I know what he knows, and he knows what I've done. He and I could have run away, but stupid Flinch caught us. Now we have no chance. But to remain silence, because one of us could be treated as a betrayer and get kill by the whole gang.

"Hey, quiet!" Marcus shouts among them. Everyone stop talking and put their attention toward Marcus. "What I cannot understand," He continues. "Is how come Cleve died while splitting up with the team, and the only people that was last seen with Mathieu, while the bomb exploded the colored cripple house, was Brandon, Kasich, Fernando and David?"

"I'm sorry to say," I excuse myself by interrupting him. "But David was found dead as well on Mathieu side."

Everybody shake their head with doubt, they could not believe David as died as well. Because among Mathieu's team he was the strongest well-built fighter ever, and fierce too.

"Than if that so," He said, as he pours a small bottle of Hennessy liquor in his mouth. "Then where is Fernando? And how come you two was caught eating food in a wood, instead of fighting in the field against our enemy, while y'all seat there in that goddamn wood consuming nutrients?"

The gang gasps as they hear these words spoken from Marcus, and they gave me the dead eye. Brandon on the other side, who could not Speak lower his gaze. He didn't want to speak up this time, because his scary self isn't smart enough to say something.

I could not understand why this information matter to them, why is it matter? What's the point of these questions? We are slave fighters, and every day we fight. It's always a matter of survival or death.

"If Fernando left no trace of blood or breath," A boy said. His dark skin tone glow as he come forward to speak. In my eyes I have doubt that that he is not less a male, he got to be a female. Even though his braided Mohawk hair appeal his face as a boy, but I doubt that he is. Since he always wears long sleeve and large shirt that is unfit for him. He seems like he got some secrets, but whatever his problem is not mine. And i never like Calvin anyway, he would not speak nor be active much. I barely forgot that he existed.

"Than he is a traitor among us." She continues. Marcus nods his head; he agrees at Calvin words. Of course he would, those wretches' people.

"Alright, boy." Marcus pounds me in the shoulder. "I'll keep an eye on you boys." He twirls his index finger through me and Brandon.

I bite my bottom lip and head to the back of one of the pick-up trucks. I lay myself there letting the hot sun breeze through my skin. Without a care I know the sun is burning my skin, but I enjoy it anyway. I enjoy the burning of pain because it kills me, not physically but emotionally.

"That's some crazy stuffs happening here." Someone says as the truck thud a little, while the person knocks its hand at it so hard. I turn my head to look who it was, then I saw Calvin with a cigarette in his mouth and a lighter in his hand while he lights up the cigar.

"I have nothing to do with Mathieu's death," I murmur. "If that's what you're coming here for."

"I didn't say that." He blows a smoke.

I lower my gaze looking at the ground, thinking why Calvin is such a way. He was nothing less but the same as me, a child. Just a child. Even though he is older than I, he is just 15, I think he should be mature enough to know good and bad. Well, I guess it depends on our human nature, to say that age and maturity doesn't matter in life. But our hearts do.

"Have you ever wonder," I whisper as the bright sun illumine in my eyes. "What is it like to be a child?"

"You are a child, and I was a child." He burst out a laugh and cough as he inhales the smoke off in his nostrils.

"Yes I know, but I mean like being completely innocent. Like being a child and plays with toys and discover or curious about the word, you know what I mean?"

He lowers his gaze and sigh, and let the puffs of smokes escape through his mouth. Then he spits, "Well that ended, didn't it?"

I nod my head. He is right, it ended it did end. He pounds my back and left me there.

At night, I pull out my sister's photo and I. And stare at those big blue eyes, she was charming and so cute. But mostly innocent. This is what I wanted to be innocent, but there is no more innocent. It all gone, it all ended.

As I think about that, I have a flashback when the Sanarina took me in their camp when I was 9 years-old. I was just small and really healthy, but mostly I was clever. I know what they were about to do to us, I know that they could not killed us, but turned us into a soldier, but what I've never thought about was that we would be trade to another.

I remember those times just like it has happened yesterday, they whooped us and threw water at us. And even burns us with hot spoon in our skins, if we would cry. They teach us how to be heartless, and forced us to sniffed coke under nose. They even gave us bows, arrows, knives, guns, and grenades. Anything that you could think of, to be trained.

They teach us how to fight, to hide under bushes and trees doing war game. But mostly what kills me most, if we failed those training test they will pull a trigger in the head of the one who fail. This is why I kept strong, I try not to fail. I even killed some of my mates, just to survive. I did it all and passes all for survival. Even though I know it was wrong to do, but to live you must do the unthinkable.

Good chance that my prayers are strong, I become a believer once in a battlefield while I was a slave for the Sanarina. A catholic priest who was protecting the people of his village, was captured and became a prisoner to the Sanarina. And I was told to guard him, and I did.

There he would bent his knees down on the floor with a rosary held tight in his hand, and he would repeat multiple prayers throughout the week. And that's when his friendship and I started to grew.

With him I felt like a child again, and my mind would imagine and puzzled those religious scriptures stories. And I would apply them in my life, but one I could not have applied is not to kill. I was used to it, and I needed it to survive but I couldn't.

However though, sadly one day the weather was gloomy. And it was my duty in the morning to go in the prisoner cell and guard him, as I went there I did not see him. I thought he had escape so I ran outside to call my chief, to tell him that the prisoner is not in his cell. But as I went to my chief in the peak of the mountain land, I saw the chief greeting his gold teeth and pointed his gun at middle age priest, while the priest plead God to let him die in peace. And that's when my chief pulls the trigger behind the head of the priest.

As I remember this sad memory, tears fall down my ears. I close my eyes tight not to think about it. I turn my head away watching the trees of the jungle and the sound of the birds chirping. It miserable to sleep in the ground since we left our tents through the mountain.

As I look at the green jungle I could visualize the priest kneeling down right in front of me, begging, praying, and a big hole bullet trace in his forehead, just where my chief has shot him dead. The blood cool down his forehead to the middle of his nose.

I close my shut again, and embrace nothingness. I say my rosary and till I fall asleep.

CHAPTER 4

"Get up! Get up!" someone keep tapping me in my sleep. I open my eyes to see who it is, then I look at the person while the sunset shine on his face. Then I realize that it is Brandon, it was him tapping me.

"What now?" I moan in my sleep.

"It's Marcus," He says in a worry voice. "He send some kids back in the city of Valcoub."

Really? Is that the reason why he come here, just to tell me an irrelevant news? I suck my teeth and lay my head back to the ground.

Brandon punches me in the arm, and pouts his lip. "Look scumbag, this is important. I think they're going back to get Fernando."

"So what?" I roll my eyes at him.

"Not only that." He puts a hand on his head. "One of us is missing, and they're searching for him."

Pshhhh! A rifle sound interrupts us. Then again the sound fire again. All suddenly I heard voices of people outside cheering.

Brandon and I look at each other and quickly got up and join the kids. They stood distance away from where I was sleeping, they bundle up together looking at something.

Brandon and I get in the middle of them, and to take a sneak look. That's when we see Marcus held his gun loading it as well, while he kneels in one leg pointing his target at a boy on the forest that is running in the forest jungle.

Marcus give another shot at the boy, but the boy did not get hit. Then he loads his gun again and shoots the boy straight in the back spiral. The boy topples on the ground, and grunts in pain.

Marcus laughs as he got his target right, Brandon and I look at each other in the eyes. He and I knew what was coming.

A boy stands beside us I ask him, why was Marcus shooting at the boy running through the jungle. He told me that's because the boy ran away while everybody was sleeping, and expect to leave us his brothers.

"Hmm…" Brandon murmurs. "That's the boy I told you about."

"Yeah," I answer him. "But you didn't tell me he was running away from us."

The boy beside us look at Brandon with a dead eye. Brandon lowers his gaze and tries to look down on the ground and smiles. But I know that smiles of his it was the weak smiles. The smiles of being afraid.

Marcus waves at us to go back to what we supposed to do in the morning, everybody turns around unexcited.

We did our morning routine which is to run in circle while Marcus and some men along with Flinch torture the boy with their feet. As they stump on him making him cry out of pain.

Later on, Claus cooked breakfast for us all to eat. We get in lines and pick up our trays and feed ourselves. As I was seating down with Brandon and two other boys which I can't recall their names. We heard a loud scream of someone crying out of pain. Of course I already knew who it was, the same boy that Marcus had shot.

The two boys left their food and run to see what else god knows what Marcus is doing to the poor child. I did the same too and then Brandon follows.

Marcus takes the boy legs and trolls him on the grassy rocky ground ramparted. Some kids were giggling, some cover their mouth in shocks, and the rebels laugh and make jokes out of it.

"Kill him!" One of the boy yells.

"Cut his throat off Master." Flinch laughs.

Marcus rolls his eyes at us and smiles in pride. He has no heart for human he will kill this boy no matter what. He doesn't need anyone permission to know how to kill this boy, because he will kill the boy anyway.

Marcus bent down grabs the boy neck and twists it. The sound of the bone crack and then the boy slightly dies.

"Holy Molly," One boy says as his eyes grew.

Everyone stood there in silence, let the sound of nature embrace.

Marcus order the rebels to bury the boy or else thrown him in the jungle. The rebels decided to throw the body in the jungle instead.

"You know," I said to Brandon as we went somewhere quiet to have a chat. "Mathieu was Marcus best right man, he always knew what was Marcus next plan, where he was going to hit, and who or what Marcus was going to sell in the black market."

"I always knew that, so."

"So, that's the reason why I killed him." I exhale deeply.

"Which got us almost in trouble." Brandon rolls his eyes. "Nope thanks."

"That's the plan, trouble." I exclaim. "I have to target all his close associates down."

Yes, that's what I wanted to, take down Marcus.

CHAPTER 5

We get in the pickup trucks and head up to Malsura, another city of Valmont. I haven't been to Malsura, I always heard that it is a place full of rich people and people who live a stable life.

"Why we going there for?" Calvin asks one of the rebels.

Louie one of the rebels who always wear a baseball cap in his head shrug to Calvin. "No idea to be honest."

"Probably he is going to get some opium." Joel laughs.

I hate this dude, Joel with his yellow teeth's. He scares me some time, I don't know why but I never feel comfortable around him. But he annoys sometimes, everything for him is a joke and I hate it.

"Quiet, Joel." Calvin kicks him in the legs playfully. Joel giggle and then got serious.

As we cross the bridges to enter Malsura, a group of military line themselves there blocking the road. When we see them we held our guns in action, but Marcus pickup truck that is in front of us stops. Then all the other pickup trucks and even ours stop too. We wait for Marcus to gives us a signal.

Marcus gets off from his pickup and stretches out his elbow, "Malsura." He chuckles. "C'mon boys, this is Marcus I'm here to see Gandolph Stacks."

One of the military soldier dress in his formal green clothes like the others, only that he has a medal badge on his shirt breast pocket. I guess he is the colonel or general or something. He goes forward to Marcus.

"Who's asking?" He asks in a shallow voice,

"Tell him that this is Marcus," Marcus answer with his traitorous smiles. "He got something I need."

"Hmm…" The military guy says under his breath. "Wait here." He orders Marcus. He went over to the side where a line of military trucks park. He opens the door and pulls out a big phone with a cord connected with the car.

"Sir, Stacks." He says in the phone.

Marcus turn his gaze at us and gave us a signal to lower our guns. Slowly we did in a nervous way, we could not understand what's going on. So we seat quiet in the car and pay attention real close.

The military guy takes a couple of minutes to talk with Stacks over the phone, I could not hear what he was saying to him since I was far. But I'm pretty sure, he seems like he untrusted Marcus.

"Alright," He hang up the phone. "Let them in." He says to the others. They split up and gave us the path to go.

Marcus get back on his truck and start driving. As we drive there the military soldiers look at us in disgust and some just roll their eyes at us. We ignore them as they did.

When we have arrived in Malrusa, loud music starts to play. The roads are quiet; people stays in their homes. And the houses are big and colorful and mostly large with big yards with mangoes trees and coconuts trees.

Finally, we arrive in an enormous mansion, it was a yellow mansion, with white windows and curtains. We park the pickup trucks outside the mansion, and a Military guy opens the gate for us to get in.

Marcus is the first to person to get in, we follow him. A military guy comes forward to Marcus and talks to him. Marcus nod his head at something he says, Brandon who is a scary cat quickly come to me.

The military guy shows us around the mansion. But most of us get distracted as we saw girls in bikinis walking around the house, with beers and alcohol held in their hands. I roll my eyes at that view, they don't seem interesting at all to me.

Brandon who is walking beside me pinch me in my arm while he grits his teeth. "Aren't they cute?"

"No, they aren't." I smirk.

"Oh, I can't stand you." He rolls his eyes.

A man with a long black hair and pointy mustache come to Marcus shaking their hands together. Marcus turns to us and say, "This Gandolph, my friend."

"Oh don't mind them," Gandolph waves his hand. "I am the mayor of this city and I got money." He laughs widely.

Gandolph is the mayor of Malrusa? And he is friended with Marcus? Then why are the military always targeting us? I don't get it.

"Do you have the Opium?" Marcus curiously asks Gandolph.

"Yeah," Gandolph taps Marcus in the shoulder, he took Marcus with him to the living room, while we go in the back of the house where the party is taking over.

They offer us drink and foods, and even let us join time to chill with some of the people there.

Flinch grabs two ladies with him and a bottle of vodka, both ladies seat on his lap and chats. Me and Brandon seat near the big pool and drink some sprites soda, a blond hair boy with a military pants walks in near us and took a seat.

"Name?" He asks.

"Brandon," Brandon introduces himself. "And Kasich." He points out to me.

"I'm Klaus," He held his hand for us to shake. I take his hand and shake it and so does Brandon.

"By the way," He says. "It sucks to be rebel boy, uhn?"

"Actually it is not what you..." Brandon explains him, but I hit Brandon in the stomach with my elbow. He grunts silently. "Damn you." He says under his breath.

"Not what?" Klaus furrows his eyebrows.

28

"Nothing." I answered him.

He raises his eyebrows at me, he knows that I was hiding something.

"Oh, alright." He smirks as he pours liquor in his soda. "I get it the brotherhood secret, right?"

"I don't know what secret are you talking." I said.

"Rebel groups are supposed to be brotherhood." He laughs. "At least that's the definition of it."

"What makes you think that we are brotherhood?" Brandon asks sharply.

"How you serve the group." He says. "People who risk their lives just to keep a group alive, that's loyalty."

"Yeah it must be," I nervously smile. "Brotherhood can never be brittle."

Klaus puts his hand inside his pants pocket, searching for something. He looks beside him and behind him to see if anyone looking or listening. But unfortunately, people seems like they're minding their own business.

"Look," He says pulling out a card from his pocket. "Take this." He held out to me.

I take the card from him and slightly put it in my jeans pocket. Brandon tries to look the other way, acting like there's nothing suspicious going on.

"I know what you boys don't know." Klaus mention. "Marcus is a man who calls everybody a brother of his, but one thing is he can sell you to the lord of death."

"Yes, I know." Brandon says. "And for your information we are slave fighter not brothers."

"I knew that," He drink his soda. "Calvin told me everything."

"What?" Me and Brandon gasp. Wait what? Calvin isn't loyal in the brotherhood? And He expects Marcus to kill a runaway.

"She's working for my boss." Klaus wiggle his eyebrows.

"Wait what?" I confusedly ask, but Brandon got in the conversation anyway. "That's a girl?"

"Yep," Klaus laugh. "She is a girl dress in a boy clothes. Beside she is undercover, she's very good at what she does."

Klaus get up and smirks, "If you boys make it alive, don't forget the number on the card. Ask for Klaus Paul." He winks at us and then turn his back and leave.

Brandon and I ran to talk to him but he disappears before we could catch a glimpse of his sight.

CHAPTER 6

Marcus got a full truck of Opium packages. We left Gandolph mansion and headed to a hotel. The hotel had a lot of people, but we kick them out of the hotel in a stern way. With rampant beating and shooting.

In the hotel Marcus who took a couple of women with him from Gandolph's mansion. Started kissing and touching in awkward ways, they laughed, pour heavy alcohol, and smoked a lot of cigars. The elders of the rebel and some brothers which are about 17 and older joins Marcus as well.

I got myself a room with a TV screen on it, and watch couple of news. I wanted to know what is happening in the country. But the news now days just report about where people should go on for safety, and nothing relevant to focus on.

I pull out my baby sister's photo out of my pocket and look at it. I wonder if she is somewhere safe, I wonder if she is happy where she is, I wonder what they've been teaching her in school, if she goes to bed at night in peace.

All these thought run in my mind, I lay in the bed thinking. Thinking about my parents. About those harsh words that they used to say to me during dinner time. What are they're doing now? What must they be saying? Who else is taking their harsh words now?

As I lay in bed, someone thud in my room door. I don't have time for all this, I don't need anyone company right now. If it's Brandon I'm definitely not going to open the door for him.

"Who is this?" I answer.

"Calvin."

I was shock that Calvin knock in my door, why would he or I don't know if I could call her a she. I shrug to myself and open the door.

"Hey," Calvin smiles.

"What's up?" I ask, and Calvin comes in.

"I know Klaus told you about me, right?" Calvin takes a seat in my bed. I nod my head at Calvin's answer.

"Now you know that I'm a girl," She finally says. "But I hope you don't tell no one about this."

"I promise." I said, not even paying attention to her.

"My mission here," She lower her gaze as she bites her bottom lip. "Is to kill Marcus."

I laugh at her regards what type of nonsense is this? To kill Marcus? I shook my head in disbelief.

"What?" She furiously asks.

"Than what are you waiting for?" I roll my eyes. "Your mission is to kill him, then make it happen. You are his closes friend and he have trust in you."

"That's what you expect." She sucks her teeth. "But it is not easy at all."

"Whatever," I wave my hand to her and lay in my bed. I look at the ceiling not caring about what Calvin as to say or must've been doing. My eyes got heavy and drowsy till it close shut.

All suddenly I could feel myself surrounded by water, the water holds me tenderly and its waves draw me in with nature. Then I open my eyes, the sun shine bright as a diamond in my eyes. I smile and embrace its nature, it feels so comfortable and mostly love.

Then a humongous whale jumps out of the water, and plunges back again. At first I became afraid, but then the whale holds me with it back. And drive me to the sky. I go higher and higher till I make it outside the earth along with the whale.

CHAPTER 7

The next morning, I woke up, I open the door after getting a good shower and put up some clothes. I went to the hall, people were looking at me, they lock their eyes on me and stares at me in suspicion as they whisper to each other.

I walk out the hotel front door, and my eyes widen as I see Fernando with his curls cover his brown eyes stands near Marcus, and Marcus hold Brandon behind the neck.

"Another traitorous kid," Marcus laughs. "You think you could have get away with it?"

"Get away with what?" I asks him as I hold on to my rifle tightly.

"Don't play dumb." Fernando burst out. "You killed Mathieu, I was right there. I saw you did it.'

"Yes I did." I cry. "I killed him, just to get into Marcus. Now let Brandon go he have nothing to do with this."

Marcus chuckles, he pulls his sharp machete and slices Brandon's right leg.

"Arghhh!" Brandon screams in pain as he collapses in the floor, while the blood from his muscles splashes on the ground.

Tears down from my eyes, and suddenly I feel enrage. In a moment I was already in front of Marcus and punch him in the stomach with force. Marcus Kick me on my waist. I topple to the ground and quickly back up again. Fernando on the other hand, hit me his elbow but I twirl my leg around his feet causes him to fall. Indeed, he did.

Brandon who was in the floor threw my rifle that had fall in the ground to me, good chance I caught the rifle within a minute I shoot at Fernando in his eyeball, he collapses and starts to scream.

I turn my rifle to Marcus, but the other kids start shooting at me. I grab Brandon who was in pain and run with him outside the gate of the hotel. The rebels and the others were shooting at me. I quickly open one of the pickup truck and push Brandon in, and I search for the keys, it seems like it already. I start the car, press my foot on the gas and starts driving.

The rebels block me and Calvin was there too, I look at her and she look at me. She nodded her head and pull out of the way, while some stood in my way. Without any hesitation I hit them with the car, not caring if they're injure or not. I just keep driving and not looking back.

CHAPTER 8

I drove far in the road of Malrusa, it's been 2 hours now since I've been driving. I don't know where I was going. Neither did I care where I am heading to. I just wanted to be free, now I am. My mind been completely blank with no worries. Thanks to the Lord that my father had teach me how to drive when I was little, since I was forced to learn to do men's work, because of what I told my parents, I do not want to be anything, but myself.

"I'm going to die." Brandon said slowly, as tears flows down his eyes.

"Shut up," I yell at him. "You're going to live."

"No, you dummy." He pouted. "I'm losing a lot of blood; I will not make it unfortunately." He touches his leg, that's still pouring out of blood.

Yes, he is right. He won't make it, but as long as he around me, he has to live.

"You can do it, Brandon."

"Look," He grunts. "If you want me to live, you either have to cut off my leg, nurse it with alcohol and then take a hot pot or whatever that goes with a fire, and press it on my injured leg. Or if can't, you either have to find a needle along with some thread and sew my leg."

I Look at Brandon as if he was crazy, I have no knowledge of what he just told me, neither am I a doctor.

"How do you know that's what you need?" I ask.

"Cause my mother is a doctor." He rolls his eyes. "I've learned a lot from her." He lowers his gaze.

I try to kept my eyes on the road but the way that Brandon was screaming out of pain make me want to pull over and help him. But I can't do that right now, not yet.

"Did you love your parents?" I ask him, trying to figure out something good to keep him alive.

"Are you kidding?" He laughs. "Which kid in the world that doesn't love their parents?"

"I don't know," I shrug. "Maybe some of those boys in Conovhi."

"Those kids," He says. "They have been forced and taking away from their homes, they're adapted to what they have been told. That does not mean that they do not love their parents. Don't you love your parents?"

I stay silent to his question until I broke it off. "The question to be ask is, do they love me?"

He chuckles as I said this. "Of course they do, they're your parents."

I shrug, "Well I don't know, they never treated me right."

Brandon stays silent throughout the road trip, and I did my best not to say anything either.

After a miles of driving in Malrusa, I decided to stop. When I saw a store near a lake house. It's called the *Healing Products*. I park the pickup truck across the store, and took Brandon with me even though he couldn't walk, I help him as I make him put an arm around my neck and I hold his waist making sure he can hold on still.

The store seems to be close, but what if there's medicines that can heal Brandon, there. I knock on the glass door nobody opens nor say anything. So I pull out my revolver and shoot at the door.

"Get out of here, you gangsters." A man voice shouts inside. It sounded like man on his 50s, but without a care I walk in anyway with Brandon.

"I need your help." I shout back. I walk inside the store there were department line of bottles with different name on it, and there seems to be statues of ancient China's dragon, the Virgin Mary, a Jesus, a book of the Quran, and few other stuffs such as the head of a goat, voodoo stuffs, and some other things that I could not even mention.

The man held a gun in his hand pointing toward me. He seems like he has a cripple leg, because he holds a crutch on his left hand to support his leg. "Why do you need my help?" He asks as he looks at Brandon from head to toe and his look seem to be concern.

"We just escaped from our master's." I explain. "My friend here has been injured. We need your help, especially a shelter to be safe."

He lowers his gun and open the store broken door glass largely to take a sneak look if anyone is with us.

"Who else is with you?" He asks.

"Nobody," Brandon grunts. "It just us. Look I'm losing a lot of blood, are you going to help me or not?"

"Alright, fine." He mumbles. "Just put him on top of the table behind the counter."

I look for the table behind the counter and lay Brandon's body there. And the man took a couple of iodine and say this will not cause Brandon's pain. He pours it on Brandon's leg in wary while Brandon trembles his body. I held Brandon's arms not to shift. The old man put sew Brandon's leg with a thread and stitches it tight.

"Who told you about me?" The old man asks me, as he points his gun at my face.

"You know what," I sight. "I'm a good sniper, if you think that I have the attention of killing you, I would have blown up your head already."

"Don't you talk to me in that tone," He said to me as he pushes me in my shoulder to grab a chair and seat.

"I'm Zachary," He coughs. "You must be?"

"Kasich," I answer him instantly. "Kasich Blond, and this is my friend Brandon."

"So Mr. Blond," Zachary raises his eyebrow. "Why did you escape from your Master?"

"Well my master," I sat in the floor beside him. "Is a cruel man. Just like all the other drug lords."

"What does he sell?"

"Opium," I slowly said. "He sell Opium."

"well," Zachary smiles. "They always said someone who have a compassion for something, can cause them to be fully enrage and then kills them."

I think about the word that Zachary just mention, compassion for something can cause rage and kills someone. Wow. I never thought of that. How come?

I hastily get up from the floor, thinking. Thinking? What am I thinking about? Suddenly a bell ring in my head. Zachary seated there in his chair confuse, he could not understand my mood.

"What is it?" He furiously says.

"Do you have a car?" I ask.

"Well I got a small Hammer," He replies. "Do you want me to drive you kids somewhere?"

"Actually, I'm going to ask you for your car keys so that I can drive somewhere."

Zachary laughs and shake his head. "You a kid it is not safe for you to drive."

"Now how did you think I got here, uhn?" I chuckle.

"I don't know," Zachary shrugs. "Maybe a ride from somebody."

"Oh no," I laugh. "I drove here all by myself."

"Oh yes he did." Brandon moan in his sleep. I laugh at him murmuring in his sleep. What a funny guy he is, but I'm actually proud that he makes it alive.

I told Zachary to watch over Brandon for me, I promised him that I will be back to take Brandon to a hospital once I finish to do an important task. So, Zachary handed me his car keys and gave me the opportunity to drive his hammer car.

CHAPTER 9

I drove downtown of Malrusa, it seems crowded there and it is hot as well, and full of traffic. I felt happy to see myself in a place with regular people, no shooting, no guns, no rebellious brothers, and no Marcus.

But I figure out that I have to do this. I went downtown to a gold pawn shop and sale the golds that Brandon and I had stolen back from Valcoub.

The pawn broker measures the golds for me, but honestly it seems like it is not enough. So, he gave me about an amount of 450 bucks cash. I got out the pawn shop all in rage, and frustrated. 450 bucks is not enough for me, it is half a share enough for Brandon, at least for his long way journey's home to his family. But for me, I wanted to settle a place for myself or just move from place to place for a good adventure.

I look around searching for a telephone booth so I can make a call. I walk a couple of blocks till I found an old use telephone booth. I grab a card on my pocket that Klaus has handed me before, and make a quick call to Klaus.

"Hello?" A female voice answers the phone.

"Hello, ma'am" I reply. "My name is Kasich Blond; can I speak to Klaus please?"

"Alright," The lady said courteously. "Hold a minute."

I wait for Klaus to get back on the line.

"Hello Kasich," Klaus voice asks over the phone.

"Hey Klaus, how you doing?"

"I'm fine," He chuckles. "I wasn't expecting your calls. Dude, did you really made it out alive from the Conovhi boys?"

"Yes, indeed." I sigh. "Look I need you to one thing for me."

"What you'd need me to do for you?"

"Can you get your associates to give me a location of where Marcus is heading to?"

A moment of silent stay over the phone, till Klaus exhale. "Look man, things are going crazy in the Conovhi brothers. But...'

"Just ask Calvin please!" I cut him off.

"Well," He says slowly. "Calvin says that Marcus will stay in Malrusa for a couple days."

"In the Hotel?"

"Nope," He says. "But in Bulzack mansion, a place he mugged just after the night you took off."

"Alright," I answer him. "Just give me the address."

Klaus gave me the address that Marcus and the Conovhi boys stays in, I quickly wrote it down on a piece of paper.

"What are you trying to do?" He asks in worry.

"I'm about to take revenge on this scumbag." I said over the phone and hang up without listening to Klaus last words.

I pull to a gas station fill up the Hammer for Mr. Zachary, got some foods for Zachary and Brandon, then head back to the store.

I park the hammer and open the glass door, all tired and sweaty I was. I went over next to the counter expecting to see Zachary and Brandon, but my jaw drop when I saw Maria. I wonder what is she doing here.

CHAPTER 10

"Hey buddy," Brandon grit his teeth widely. "Look who is here."

"Hi," Maria comes toward me. "Kasich." She smiles. My heart skips a beat when she approaches me. I could not help but smile.

"Why so nervous?" She asks.

I nod my head. "Nothing." I said timidly. "What? What are you doing here?"

"Just came to visit my grandpa." She grabs my hand. "Papa." She calls out to Mr. Zachary.

Zachary take the food out of my hand and said, "Brandon told me." He smirks at me.

Throughout the evening Brandon, Maria, Mr. Zachary and I did a little chat about how life in Conovhi, and mostly about Marcus.

I told Brandon about my plan for the night, that I was about to sneak inside the Bulzack mansion and destroy Marcus drugs.

So, later that night. Zachary gave me a couple gasoline, grenades, and new bullets for my rifle. He was so worry about me, but I told him that he didn't have to be, that is my live. A slave fighter, and when a slave revolts against his master nothing can't stop him from doing except for death.

CHAPTER 11

I drove to the address that Klaus has given me during the night, to the Bulzack's mansion. It has been a long night for me and I have to do my task. Brandon's leg injury stays in my mind; I could not forget about it. Obviously, it irritates me. I cannot see myself just there and do nothing about it.

I listen to a couple of American rap music in the car radio, as I drive on the road. It boosts up the heat in my vein, and brings me courage. I sing the lyrics of the Tupac song, *Hail Mary*. Yes, this song. It is perfect. This song will cause Marcus to cry on the shoulder of his Opium drugs, and his violent lifestyles.

Finally, I arrive in front of the Bulzack's mansion, I got off the car. Take some of my equipment with me. The gate and the walls outside the mansion are a few meters high. This will be difficult for me to climb this wall, but first before I could figure out how to climb this wall, I need to know if there's anyone guarding the gate on the inside.

I grab Zachary's power drill behind the car, and walk behind the mansion's wall. I put my ear close to the wall, listening instinctively to what's going on behind it. Although, I could not hear anything nor anybody's voice. So, I use the power drill making a hole on the wall. With my foot I smash the hole into pieces with a carjack from the hammer till it creates an alley.

I jump inside the alley, and step in the yard behind the mansion. I sneak behind the bushes and the coconut trees, seems like everybody is sleeping. I walk into the garage where the pickup trucks park in. I search for Marcus truck's license plate. *H3299M*, I passed a couple of pickup trucks until I find *H3299M*. I pour the gasoline that Mr. Zachary had handed me, and lavishly shower it with the gasoline. I go behind his pickup truck making sure that the Opium are there. Fortunately, they are. They're cover with a rug on top of them, I bitterly laugh. I turn on my lighter and threw it on the Opium.

The order of the Opium invades the air, but I cover my mouth not to inhale the scent.

The fire starts to burn the truck, I quickly take a step back and the pickup truck blew up. As the truck shatter into pieces and hit the other trucks, the other trucks make siren noises. Waking up everybody and even the neighbors beside the mansion I think.

Behind the curtain of the windows of the house, I could see lights turn on and people are running in panic.

"Go I got this!" Someone voice yells out.

I turn my gaze where the sound of the voice was screaming, then a smile appears on my face. It was Calvin, she was running to me.

"Let's go." I grab Calvin arm. I was surprise to see her out and let her curls fall to her neck.

"Marcus founds out that I am a girl." She cries.

I raise an eyebrow at her, I knew that Marcus will found out somehow. You can't hide from him, no one can.

"So, I think this is the moment that we have to run." I pull her, but she pushes my hand away. "I have to kill him tonight, I have to."

"How are you going to do that?"

"You go hunt Flinch in the basement," She orders me. "And I go kill Marcus."

"Calvinnnnn!" Marcus yells out from the roof window. "I'm going to kill you with my bare hand you're lying witch."

I push Calvin to the ground and make Marcus see me finally, make him see that I am the one causing all this trouble.

"Your drugs are burned now," I laugh loudly as I could. "You must be in rage now my master."

Flinch jumps out from his window with an arrow and bow. Before he got the chance to hit it, I threw a grenade at him, he yells out of panic. But the grenade blew up with his leg.

"Ahhhh." He screams.

Calvin tries to grabs her rifle, but I ran before she got the chance to. I went over to Flinch and blow up his brain without any hesitation.

I ran to the hammer quickly, I fasten my seatbelt and starts driving in full speed. A slight tears slide under my eyes; I realize that I shouldn't have leave Calvin there. But she refused to come with me anyway.

I drove to the store, and when I got there I didn't see Brandon, Maria, and Zachary. I search everywhere for them, but there is no place for them to be found. Only the blood of Brandon that stick on the floor.

CHAPTER 12

"Brandon!" I yell out in the street. "Zachary, Maria." No one answer, no one says anything either. So, I guess that I am here all alone in this soothed street yelling out people names.

I went down to the same telephone booth that I went earlier, I gave a call to Klaus.

"Hello Klaus?" I sob on the phone. All suddenly, it starts to rain with thunder that lightened in the dark sky.

"Kasich?" He answers over the phone. "Did Calvin make it?"

"I don't know." I bang on the booth. "But I think I lost Brandon."

"What?" He bursts out. "Look I'm going to tell my boss to locate them right now."

"Can you just come over here, instead." I stumble on my words. "Don't come with the military come by yourself, alright?"

I gave him the location of the store. I went back to the store, and waited there while I look at some books and examine those statues.

Then all the sudden, I heard the door open. I quickly get up to see who it is, then I was stunned to see Klaus in his full military clothes.

"Who did you leave Brandon with?" He asks as he took a seat beside me. "An old man along with the old man's granddaughter."

"Where could've they gone to?" He sighs.

I shrug my shoulder; I just feel like crying but doesn't have the guts to.

A laugh outside interrupts the silence that I have with Klaus. The laugh seems like a girl laughing, swiftly the glass door open then Maria holds a grocery bag on her hands as she soaks wet. And Zachary holds Brandon by the waist while Brandon hold two crutches to help himself with his injured leg.

Really? I sight. Why would they leave this place make it seem like something had happen to them? Jesus, I was worried for nothing.

"Seems like your friends are ok." Klaus taps my shoulder.

Brandon rolls his eyes as he sees Klaus, and Zachary and Maria goes in front of Klaus and introduces themselves.

"What happened to your leg?" Klaus asks Brandon.

"That moron Marcus," Brandon sucks his teeth. "He sliced my leg with a machete." He gestures his hands to show Klaus.

"Seems like this guy Marcus," Maria held me and Klaus a bowl of rice. We thank her and eat the food that she brought, as she continues to speak. "Is a man that you have to eliminate yourself."

"Yes, definitely." Klaus mumbles as he chews his rice. "You know I tried to get my some of my military men to get close to him, but it seems impossible."

"Well you got those boys here." Zachary pulls a glasses out of the counter. "With them anything is possible just to blow this guy head off."

"No," I interrupt. "I got to do this for myself. For my sake."

Klaus cellphone rings putting us all into a silence, Klaus looks at the number and pick it up quickly. "Hello, this is Klaus. How can I help you?" He courteously said over the phone.

Klaus listen to the caller's voice for a couple of minute and slowly drop the phone on the floor, while he stood there numb and tears flow down his eyes.

"What is it, Klaus?" Brandon asks in panic.

"Calvin is dead." He sobs as he go down on the floor. Maria and I went over to him and caresses him.

"How do you know?" I empathically asks him, as my heart start to be confuse and sad as well.

"We spies them with camera on the Bulzack's mansion." He cries while tears just drop like rain in his eyes.

CHAPTER 13

The following day, I woke up seeing myself in the bed after a sorrowful night. It was sad and still mournful to learn that Calvin has died. I mean how could she? Calvin was very strong and intelligent among us. I knew it so well that she couldn't hide her secret away from Marcus. No one can hide from him, nobody can.

Near my bed there place a cup of coffee, some bread and eggs. I grab my breakfast and eat it. Then, I went to the bathroom and do my hygiene. Later that morning, I go on the lake behind Zacharay's store. Despite the fact that I already took a shower, I wanted to go on for a swim.

I plunge in the water and starts swimming, I felt happy each times I move my legs and arms for support. But while I was swimming something didn't seem right. Something soft and big is brushing my feet, I became frighting and curious. I wonder what is it.

I go under the water just to take a look, while I hold my breathing. Then, I was astonish and fright as the same time to see a big whale, just like the one in my dream. I quickly got off the water and grab my clothes to run, but Maria came in running toward me as she gesture her hands for me to calm down.

"There's a big whale in there," I push her on the elbow to go back. "You can't play in the lake, go."

"Cool down." She giggles. "It's hope."

What? Hope? Is she okay? I cannot understand her right now. I just told her there's a whale under the water and she is talking about hope.

I stood there confuse. But she takes my hand and come close to the lake as she whistle, and the big whale jumps out the water as it twist it tails in the air and fall back into the water.

"That's hope," Maria come close to the lake. "He save my brother's life."

"How?" I curiously ask. "How could a whale save a human."

"Far behind the lake," She explains. "A group of rebel just like Marcus' group. They chase my brother like a dog for not accepting the offer of being a slave fighter, then he jumped in the ocean located behind the lake, he couldn't swim. So he almost drown, and those rebels wouldn't dare to go in the ocean to save him. So, he was drowning no one wouldn't dare to save his life, so this creature magically elevate him in the air and slightly place him on the ground gently. Then, the rebel ran away and never come back. That's how we adopt him."

"Really?" I ask.

The whale pick it head out of the water wailing, I come close to it and caresses it head slowly. And it sniffs my fingers while wailing. All the sudden it felt funny and soft, even ticklish. I could not help but smiles, this whale makes me smile.

"Why you name it hope?" I ask Maria.

She bent her head unable to look me in the eye, but seems like she's sad. As if she have a hole on her chest that is killing her.

"Maria," I said to her, while I gave her tight hug.

"My brother is in the military," She sobs. "He haven't come home for two years neither do we ever heard his voice or heard any news from him. This is why we called the whale hope."

The whale wails again as Maria cried out of pain. After Maria as wiped her tears the whale goes back under the lake, like it just disappear.

"I'm going to kill this man!" A familiar voice screams outside by the store.

"C'mon Klaus do not go out there and kill yourself." Another familiar voice mention in order to calm Klaus.

Maria and I look at each other, we knew too well whose voice that belong. We both run leaving the lake and go in front of the store.

Brandon with his damage leg, holds his crutch standing in front of the glass door yelling out Klaus name that is crossing the street all in rage and mad.

CHAPTER 14

"I'm going to kill him!" Klaus screams on top of his lung. "I'm going to kill that devil."

"Calm down son," Mr. Zachary runs across the street trying to grab Klaus by the shirt to calm him down. "Yes, you will get the chance to." Finally Zachary hold Klaus by the shirt, but Klaus push Zachary away on the shoulder in discourtesy.

Brandon who stood by the glass door have a small revolver in his pocket, I grab it from him without even looking and shot three bullets in the air. Then, everyone got quiet. But Maria scarcely go behind Brandon since she's not use to those gunshots easily.

"Quiet Klaus." I yell at him. "You cannot just go ahead and kill someone evil like that. First of all, you must think about the others." I said on top of my lungs so everyone could hear me. "We must fight for them and give them justice. Cause no one deserve to be a slave fighter and not living a good life. No child should hold a gun in his hand and looses his or her innocence by killing people. We are human beings, and it's time to fight the devil and not keep letting the evil win over us. We must not and not let this happen ever again."

"You say that like some of them did not turn evil." Klaus grabs me on my collar shirt, as his breathing becomes heavy.

"I know," I answer slowly. "I know some of them turn evil, but they're been psychologically control, they're psychologically weak, and psychologically looses their spiritual substance of being human."

"Then what about your parents?" Brandon interrupts.

Zachary and Maria held hands together and wait for me to answer Brandon's question, but I decided to lower my gaze and not responding as go inside the store.

Later on, Brandon came by to me after calming Klaus's anger. He tries to apologize to me, but I turn my back not looking at him. "You know, you some lovely parents, right?"

"Yes I do know," He smirks. "But the thing is before I die, I will like you to get happiness."

"I will." I furiously answer.

He stays silence for a moment and then continues. "What I mean is to learn how to forgive your parents."

"That's not happiness." I suck my teeth at him.

Brandon's put a hand over my shoulder, "Think about your little sister, I'm sure you would not like her to be suffering like Maria's without a brother." He says.

"She have other brothers." I said slowly, as I try not to think of my sister.

"But she might loves you more than the others." He shrugs. "You may never know. And beside as you grew older your parents will starts to treat you like they're supposed to, nothing is meant to stay like we sees it right now." He taps my shoulder then leave.

So, I guess that Maria told him about her brother, uhn.

"Are you alright, boy?" Zachary's voice says from behind.

"Yeah," I nodded. "I think so."

"Brandon told me about how you don't like your parents, you know." He took a seat beside me.

"Oh my god." I sight in frustration. "He can't keep his mouth shut."

"He wasn't trying to," Zachary lowers his gaze. "Actually, I told him about Maria's brother who made it to the military and never came back."

"Yeah she told me about that one," I answer him. "Plus the whale."

"Did you see it?" He asks. "The whale?"

"Yes indeed."

Zachary talks about the story of the whale and how every time that they wish for something, the whale brings them luck. At first, I was uncertain about it, but then I decided to go over the lake and talk to the whale myself.

The big whale pop up its head out the lake and looks into my deep blue. It creeps me out when it does that, but I feel like I could say anything and think of anything.

"I want to kill Marcus," I lower my gaze as the whale wails. "I hope I have the courage to do it."

Tears flow down my eyes as I think about my sister, I wish I get my vengeance from Marcus for the sake of my sister. "I heard that you have the power to make wishes come true, I wonder if it's true. Only if you were able to talk you could have answer that."

After I have talked to the whale, I went over to the counter inside the store where Klaus seat behind the counter and do some over thinking issues. I interrupts him in his thoughts of sadness and told him to drive Brandon to an hospital. Because Brandon's condition could get serious later, beside even though Zachary sew his leg with some thread and cover the wound, I doubt that the wound is not clean enough.

Klaus agrees with me and promises to sent Brandon to an hospital where he can get recover. Both of us, Klaus and I talk to Brandon about it and the problems that he could be facing later base on his condition. He totally agrees with me.

CHAPTER 15

Klaus did what I told him to, but before Klaus took off with his car to drive Brandon to an hospital. I walk over to his car where Brandon tries to gather himself comfortably in the passenger seat.

"Hey, buddy." I pad him in the shoulder. "You're going to be alright." I smile wide to him.

He shook his head with doubt. "I think the doctors might do a surgery on my leg."

"So, what's wrong with that?" I ask.

"Oh c'mon." Brandon rolls his eyes. "I might get a fifty percent chance of surviving this surgery."

"It's a surgery in the leg, not in the heart." I said punching him in shoulder, as I laugh. "And you can't possibly think that the doctors are going to practice a surgery on you."

"Yeah," He smirks. "True that. But if they do and I don't make it alive somehow." He pulls out a letter from his jeans pocket and hand it over to me. "Please, give this to my mother, and tell her that I love her and father too."

I take a look at the letter and curiously look in the back of it. There it says *From Brandon Azahazi to Sara and Niyongo Azahazi*, and it mention the address name next the name of the two people.

"You wrote to them?" I stammer.

"Indeed, I have for God sake." He cries. "I miss them daily."

I feel like crying with him, but I don't want him to see those tears. I realize that I miss my family too, despite all the things that they have done to me. But something inside me wanted me to forgive them. And each time as I think about them and their deeds, the more that miss them.

"I miss mine too, I think." I said to him slowly.

Brandon smiles to me widely as if he became proud of me. "You should, I know you do." He punches me back in my shoulder laughing.

I look at Klaus who already have his hand on wheel. He tries to breath in and out, trying relaxes himself. "Buddy," I said to him. "Drive him safe, ok." He nods his head as he agrees to my word. "You can count on me." He answer.

I gave Klaus a handshake and along with Brandon. Maria and Zachary went over to them and says their goodbyes ans wishes to see them again in the future. Then, Klaus took over the road with Brandon, and I just stand in front of the store with Zachary and Maria waving our hands goodbye.

CHAPTER 16

Zachary went to the guns store, brought some guns and some sharp knives. Then, he gave them to me to train myself with them behind the lake near the ocean, but a swamp.

However though, I don't mind training in the swamp. Beside it is quiet there and it seems like a good place to meditate myself.

I threw punches and throw kicks non-stop, I did some sit ups and some push ups. I ran and ran just like my old routines in the Conovhi gang.

Maria cook some foods for me and her grandpa. I ate with them and watch the news from television.

Later on, Zachary gave me his car keys and some of the guns that he brought me along with grenades, and some punching gloves to protect my knuckles.

Zachary and Maria walk me to the driver's seat and put the weapons behind the car. I open the door and hop up in the chair. "God speed my boy." Zachary gives me a tight hug and then Maria came to me with a smile.

"Come back here, alive. Please." She lowers her gaze and a drop of tears fall down from her eye. I wipe the tears swiftly from her eyes as she weep.

"I will," I whisper to her. "I will make it alive. I promise." Then, she come to face and slowly presses her lips on mine. I did the same too, as I suck her bottom lip softly and sweet. I feel like kissing her forever but I couldn't. Then, she releases her lips from mine and cover her lips with her hand as she giggle.

Zachary who saw this groans and clear his throat. I lower my eyes and smile. Therefore, it is kind of uncomfortable to kiss a girl in front of her parents or her grandparents. It is not suitable to do it, but it is the right time too because I might never seen her again.

Maria go next to her grandfather and waves their hands to me as they say goodbye. I wave back to them and take off.

I drive in the road and start to have flashback of all the things that the Sanarina and the Conovhi had done to me. I listen to some music and drive. I stop near a telephone booth and put some coins, and call Klaus cellphone.

"Hello," He answers the phone with a sobbing voice.

"Hey, Klaus." I said over the phone. "What happen? Why are you crying?"

"I'm sorry." He weeps. "But the Conovhi has killed Brandon inside the hospital."

"What?" I exclaim in panic over the phone, while my hands tremble. "How did this happen."

"They have a spy." He says. "Ever since you left after attacking the hotel, they've been tracking you through every step and so they have track down Brandon."

I stood there numb and the phone slip from my hand. My breathing starts to become heavy as I punch my the phone booth with my fist.

I curse under my breath and hop up in the car and drove back to Zachary store. When I arrive to the store the glass door stay open, I got inside in the store in a hurry and what I saw with my bare eyes seem shocking to me and unbelievable.

My legs felt weak as I collapse on the floor, and I start to weep and broken inside just seeing Zachary's dead body lies on the floor lifeless. But what mostly tragic is those bullets on his chest. They weren't only one or two, but 16 bullets wounds on his stomach and chest, and even in the heart.

However though, his eyes was open. They were not flinching, but they're just paralyze. With my fingers I close them slowly and weep. Then, I got up to look for Maria as I cry, but she was no where to be found. I walk behind the lake near the ocean, near the swamp, and I even jump on the water just to check on the big whale as I swim, but the whale was no where to be found as well.

I run to the sidewalk six or seven blocks away from the store without even stop to a telephone. I quickly put some coins and punch Klaus number.

"Hello." He said in a gloomy voice.

"It's me again," I sob on the phone. "Zachary is dead, and Maria is missing."

"I'm going in." He says.

"Going where?"

"In Malrusa's Valley." He weeps. "I'm going to kill Marcus."

"No," I said to him. "Leave that to me."

I ask for the hospital that Brandon is in, and told him to tell the Doctors not to remove Brandon's body till I come. He agree with me and I took Zachary's hammer and drove for about an 1hour and 45 minutes.

I got inside of the hospital with a rush. I ask for Brandon's room to the register table, the nurse told me it's room 213. There was a lot of police officer inside the hospital and even the military guys were there. I try to rush to get inside the elevator, but one military guy stops me in front of the elevator door.

"Why are you going to see Brandon?" He asks in a shallow voice.

Me whose body was sweating to death wonder why most of the military dudes always have a shallow. I roll my eyes at him and just answer him. "I'm a friend of Klaus, can you please let me in?"

"I'm sorry kid, but this is a murder scene." He babbles.

"Look, can you just call Klaus please." I burst.

He puts his index and finger up telling me to hold on, then he dial on the phone. Then says. "Hello Klaus."

Klaus and the guy talks for about three minutes on the phone, then the guy turn off his cell phone and look me up. "You can go now." He smirks.

Without even thanks the guy the elevator opens and I hop up inside the elevator.

As the elevator go up with me, I weep in tears. I wanted to punch something, something fragile maybe.

Finally the elevator open in the second floor, I got off from the elevator and look for the room 214. Till I came face to face with Klaus and two police officers and three military guys stand in front of a room where a white sheet cover a body inside.

I stop there, my eyes fix in the body that is cover. Suddenly I felt weak, not physically but mentally weak.

"I'm so sorry." Klaus tries to tap my shoulder.

Without even looking at him, I got inside the room and seat in the bed beside the dead body. I wish it is not Brandon, please God tell me it is not him. I slowly take off the sheet from the dead face, and what I saw hit me right in my chest but mostly in my heart. I could not help but cry, and I cry loudly as I could.

Brandon's body became pale and cold. And his neck have a mark of knife that reap his skin.

"The spy came here while he was sleeping just after the doctor gave him a serum." Klaus explains from behind. "I went downstairs to buy some chocolate milk for him since he told me that he didn't like the hospital food. And when I came back and opened the door, he was slice in the neck and its seem like he was struggling. Cause his body was found in the floor."

"What is it like loosing Calvin?" I ask.

"It's like hell for me," He sniffs. "She was like my sister. She was only seven when my mother brought her in Valmont with us, she was just an innocent girl who came from Africa, and she had no family except mine."

"I understand." I sight. "I understand."

Without hesitation I walk out of the hospital and hop up in the hammer car. Now let the vengeance begin. If ever Maria is with them, I am going to get Maria and kill Marcus.

CHAPTER 17

5:45 PM I arrive in front of the Marulsa's Valley, I heard it is a popular one and someone that I want to perish forever.

I got off the car, and walks inside the grassy valley. There it seems a lot of mountain. So I decided to walk, after climbing mountains to mountains I came to face a forest on top of the valley.

However though, there seems to be a lot of noise inside the forest. With my sweating body, I took off my shirt and my shoes. I sneak behind the trees to take a look at the people who were screaming. My eyes are stun to see the Conovhi brothers in a seance in front of a fire. They were dancing and shouting like people chanting witchcraft. But their leader wasn't here Marcus.

Slowly I pull out my grenades unbuckle it, and threw it at their direction.

A boy scream, "Grenade! Grenade." They all panic, before they have the time to run the grenades blows them up. I hide behind the tree that was kind of far from them. And cover my ears with my fingers as the grenades blew off.

A bunch of boys game with grenades and starts to shoot. Since the tree is strong enough the bullets could not come through, so I stay there letting waste their bullets.

Then as their bullets had wasted, I pull out a bow and some arrow that I found in Zachary's bedroom and shoot at them one by one with speed. Then, they all collapse on the ground lifeless.

Suddenly, everything seems quiet. I know that Marcus was there so I stood in my ground waiting for him.

"Marcus!!" I yell on top of my lungs. "Come here and fight me like a man."

Then someone behind the branches of the trees in the forest came near me facing me. It was Marcus. He laughs as he see me.

"You know," He chuckles. "I always knew you got the devil inside of you."

"Where's the girl?" I ask with anger.

"What girl Mr. Blonde?" Marcus shrugs as he held a sword in his hand. Then all suddenly, it starts to rain. Not slowly but rapidly rain. "There is no girl here Kasich."

"Don't play dumb." I shout. "You sent your spy to kill my friends, and now you act like there's no girl."

He smirks and shook his head as if something was funny. He says, "Throughout your journey my spies as only told me that you were in town with old man,

Brandon, and Calvin's adoptive brother, Klaus. There was no girl."

What? He think he is smart? I know Maria is here I have to find her. "Give me Maria!"

"There is no Maria," He laughs. "I guess that you're having some type of illusion."

"I'm not having no..." He throws a cellphone near my feet, then says. "Call Klaus, tell him if he have seen the girl that you asking for."

I raise an eyebrow as the rain drop on my face. I do not understand? Is Klaus is involve in this quarrel too?

I pick up the phone slowly as I point my gun at him, and I dial Klaus's number. The phone rings a couple of second as I look straight in Marcus eyes, till Klaus picks it up.

"Hello, Klaus." I say over the phone.

"Hey," He answers. "Did you kill him?"

"No, not yet." I sigh. "He is standing right in front of me. Actually, I was searching for Maria, I wonder if you have seen her since Marcus told me to ask you."

"What? Maria?" Klaus curiously ask over the phone.

"Yes Klaus, Maria."

"I'm sorry buddy." He said slowly. "But I don't know who is Maria."

Suddenly I was in shock. How come Klaus said there is no Maria when we have spent some days with her along with her Grandpa.

"But she is Zachary's granddaughter," I stammer. "Don't you remember when she spent day in the store with us."

"I think you are confuse." He answered. "Zachary didn't have a granddaughter with us in the store, there was no girl at all. It was only me, you, Brandon and Zachary in the store throughout the day. And are you okay?"

The phone slip from my hand as my eyes flinches at Marcus. Marcus laughs and whispers. "I think you been a little over thinking lately." He smirks as he presses is long sword. "How about you let me fix that for you." He held is sword in the air.

I close my eyes thinking of the catholic priest that my chief from the Sanarina had shot. And pull the trigger. Then, I open my eyes to see Marcus with a bullet in his head and topples to the ground.

I faint in the ground and everything goes pitch black. There was no one, and nothing to see.

CHAPTER 18

Slowly a light illuminate the darkness. The light was bright and pure as it shine in my eyes. I let my eyes open slowly, then the first person I see is a little girl in a blue dress, with pink lips, and blue eyes like mine smiling at me. She looks just like me, and she caresses my forehead.

"Where am I?" I ask her.

With an angelical voice she answer. "You are in Morentzo, in a hospital near home."

I flinch my eyes to see much clearly, but mostly to understand where I am. "I can't be." I whisper.

"Brother," She smiles. "There's nothing to worry about. You are a hero."

I rub my eyes to see her clearly and the room. Yes she was right, I am in an hospital, and there was serum and those needles in my arms. She is right. But am I really in Morentzo.

I lift up my head to look, and there stood my grandmother Nola and my two older brothers in her arm. I felt in shock, I wonder if I was dreaming or not.

Maybe I should pinch myself, but that wasn't necessary to do. My two brothers came running to me in my bed and tickles me as they giggle in tears of joy. Then, I realize that it is real. I'm not dreaming.

My grandmother Nola kisses my forehead and my sister gave me a tight hug as she weep of joy.

"My brother," She whispers while crying. "I thought I lost you."

"You didn't." I whisper back to her. "I am here, I am here for you love." I kiss her forehead as she keeps on crying.

Then, I turn my head to see my mother with her messy hair bond, with tears in her eyes while my father hold her tight as he weeps with her.

I look at them as every one release themselves from me. Both of my parents came up to me in tears afraid to touch me.

"I am so sorry honey." My mother kneel down near me. "I have think about you all the time, ever since you left I could not forgive myself through everything that I have done to you. Kasich, we are your mother and your father hope you forgive us."

I turn my head not wanting to see them. Then I heard my father says, "I am such a terrible father." He burst up crying as he ran out of the room in tears.

Few weeks later, Klaus came to visit me in my home in dinner night with my family. My father told him to join us for dinner, he was happy the day with me.

"I couldn't be more proud of a hero like you." He says to me.

"I am not hero." I said to him. "I fight to survive."

He nods his at me, he tap me on the shoulder and says. "The president wants to honor you in the presence of killing one of the biggest drug lord of Valmont, Marcus."

I look down at my food, I don't know if I'm suppose to be happy or unhappy. Therefore, I could still remember my troubles of being a slave to him, and mostly to old chief in the Sanarina.

"What about the Sid," I ask. "The drug lord of the Sanarina?"

Klaus look down at his food too and smile proudly as everyone in the table wait for him to say something.

"He also have been killed too," He smirks. "By a girl name Maria, who was his sex slave. She killed with a knife straight in the heart."

"Maria?" I ask in surprise. Klaus says yes with a confuse face, then he realizes when I ask him about the girl named Maria.

"I remember you ask me for her," He said in amazement. "Before you killed Marcus, you ask me about a girl name Maria which you haven't even met."

"Really," My brother Tristan interrupts in a curious. "How did that happen?"

"A Connection." Lela says. "A sort of unfinished deed that you were suppose to do. Let me guess, a parallel self connection."

"Hmmm..." My mother clear her throat. "What is that?"

"It's like two humans who live in the same place," She explains. "They both think they met somehow in dreams like a connection, or visualize each other. Than they both did something that one could not finish for them."

Lela told me she learned this through some science book. I was impressed by that. Later on, I asks Klaus where is Maria. He told me she is now living with her brother in the United State. I was shock and happy to hear the news. Finally, I realize that maybe I was having some type of illusion but one that is one of a hell of illusion that turns out to be real.

The President of Valmont had honor me with a gold medal chain in the palace along with Klaus by my side.

After being honored, I went to Brandon house to visit his parents there. I handed them the letter that Brandon had gave me to send to them. They cried in tears to the fact of loosing Brandon their youngest son after I learned that Brandon had two siblings. They thanked me with all their love and even open the door of their hearts to keep in touch with me at all time. Because to them I was a hero for them, and mostly to their son.

7 years later has passed ever since my struggle of being a slave fighter. Valmont still suffering under the laws of Drug lord, but little not like it was before. And the government of Valmont now finally embraces the people of Valmont for once. However, the country was still not at piece, because the world is not. But achievement has been trained or gained in the country.

Now I am a student at the University of Oxford, England and studying the laws of politic there. I realize that, this it is what I wanted to do with my life to become a politician. One that could speak for others, and maybe one day I could speak for the people of Valmont despite the fact my childhood innocence has ended longtime ago. But mostly what remain in my heart is Brandon, he was such a great friend and I could never forget that. From him I have learn how to forgive my parents, and move on with life for good and for all.

Printed in the United States
By Bookmasters